LOUISVILLE

GAME

The River City

THE RIVER CITY

T

GAME 2

SIMON & SCHUSTER
BOOKS FOR YOUNG READERS

NEW YORK | LONDON
TORONTO | SYDNEY

PREGAME RECAP

After their missing father's funeral, three kids—Griffith, Ruby, and Graham Payne—are given a battered, old baseball by their father's brother, Owen. He also tries to give the siblings some advice about the ball. Before he can finish, their mother—angered by something Owen has done—rushes the family off. But Uncle Owen promises to send more information via letter.

Two of the pieces of advice Uncle Owen does manage to give—"always be together" and "see the things that others don't"—begin to make sense once the Paynes hit the road with the Travelin' Nine, because when Griffith, Ruby, and Graham hold the baseball together, weird things happen on the ball field, things that only the kids and the members of the Travelin' Nine can see.

This makes Uncle Owen's third piece of advice, a warning that unspeakable danger lies ahead, seem that much more ominous. So when Uncle Owen's letter finally arrives, tattered and a little bloody, Griffith fears the worst and decides to wait until they are on a steamboat to Louisville, Kentucky, to show the letter to Ruby.

Acknowledgments

A special thanks goes out to Penny, Paul, Josh, and Jillian—our Louisville connection—for helping with some of the research that went into this book, and a big huzzah goes to the vintage baseballists in Cincinnati for their inspiration for this series.

SIMON & SCHUSTER BOOKS FOR YOUNG READERS
An imprint of Simon & Schuster Children's Publishing Division
1230 Avenue of the Americas, New York, New York 10020
This book is a work of fiction. Any references to historical events, real people, or real locales are used fictitiously. Other names, characters, places, and incidents are products of the authors' imagination, and any resemblance to actual events or locales or persons, living or dead, is entirely coincidental.
Text copyright © 2007 by Phil Bildner and Loren Long
Illustrations copyright © 2007 by Loren Long
SIMON & SCHUSTER BOOKS FOR YOUNG READERS is a trademark of Simon & Schuster.
Book design by Jessica Sonkin and Dan Potash
The text for this book is sent in Century 731 BT.
The illustrations for this book are rendered in charcoal.
Manufactured in the United States of America
2 4 6 8 10 9 7 5 3 1
CIP data for this book is available from the Library of Congress.
ISBN-13: 978-1-4169-1864-6
ISBN-10: 1-4169-1864-7

6411

To Roberto Clemente,

Bob Costas,

Doris Kearns Goodwin,

Fay Vincent,

George Will,

and all the other

believers in baseball

and keepers of the game.

—P. B.

To my father,

William G. Long,

who introduced me

to the Big Red Machine.

I'd still rather go to a ball game

with you than anyone.

—L. L.

CONTENTS

CHAPTER 1
THE LETTER 1

CHAPTER 2
TRAVELING DOWN THE OHIO RIVER 8

CHAPTER 3
MY JOURNAL, BY RUBY PAYNE 16

CHAPTER 4
UNABLE TO SLEEP 22

CHAPTER 5
ON THE STREETS OF LOUISVILLE 32

CHAPTER 6
THE RIVER CITY SHOWDOWN 40

CHAPTER 7
CHURCHILL DOWNS 51

CHAPTER 8
STUNNED DISBELIEF 57

CHAPTER 9
THE GAME BEGINS 72

CHAPTER 10
THE RUBE WADDELL SHOW 80

CHAPTER 11
HORSES, HORSES, EVERYWHERE! 85

CHAPTER 12
LEARNED IN LOUISVILLE 96

CHAPTER 13
BEN BRUSH! 113

CHAPTER 14
COMING BACK! 129

CHAPTER 15
THE NINTH INNING 137

CHAPTER 16
NOW OR NEVER 150

CHAPTER 17
THREE OUTS TO GO 157

CHAPTER 18
THE VICTORY BURGOO 170

CHAPTER 19
SCRIBE SHARES 178

CHAPTER 20
THE ABSOLUTE TRUTH 186

★ THE LETTER ★

uby stood by the ship's boiler and removed Uncle Owen's letter from the tattered envelope. The tips of her fingers tingled.

She already knew what it said. But now she was seeing the words with her own eyes.

Beware the Chancellor

Ruby knew who the Chancellor was. Everybody who lived anywhere near Washington, D.C., in 1899 knew who the Chancellor was. He was a businessman who craved only money and power. But no one *wanted* to do business with him. Everyone tried to steer clear of the Chancellor; everyone avoided crossing his path. He was someone the grown-ups spoke of with hushed voices, which was the reason all the kids at school talked about him the way they did. They had made him something of a legend. Some even said he had evil powers, but Ruby and Griffith had never believed those claims.

"There had to have been more," Ruby said to her older brother, who stood by the engine room door. "Maybe another page."

Griffith peeked down the corridor to make sure no one was coming and then nodded. "That's what I think too."

When the letter had arrived, Griffith's heart had skipped a beat. What had happened to it? Tattered. Crinkled. Smudged. Even partially opened. How did it get that way? It looked as though it had been through a war.

Just like their baseball.

After examining the smudges more closely, Griffith's fears had deepened. The rust-colored stains looked like blood. Had something happened to Uncle Owen?

Ruby turned the letter over. "What's this?"

"What's what?"

Ruby stepped around the storage containers to Griffith. "I think there's something else written here."

Griffith checked the hall again, then took the paper from his sister. He held it to the light dangling from the beam above his head and read the tiny inscription scribbled along the edge.

He mustn't learn of the baseball

Griffith's breaths quickened. The beads of sweat, which had already formed at his temples because of the heat, now ran down

his cheeks and chin, and along his neck. He quivered, just like he had when he first read the letter only a few hours before back in Cincinnati.

His mind flitted to last autumn, when his mother had taken Ruby and him to the market. As word had spread that the Chancellor and his men were present, Griffith had felt the chill in the air. He could still see the fathers nervously searching the crowd and the mothers holding their little ones closer,

Then Griffith had spotted *him*. It was only a fleeting glimpse, and for the most part, he was shielded from view by his men. Wearing those perfectly ironed navy suits with the pink pocket squares, they always surrounded him. The Chancellor was protected, untouchable.

Beneath the man's wide-brimmed hat, Griffith had seen a colorless, almost *inhuman* face. Like that of a cobra. Then, the Chancellor had turned and plowed through the crowd, an unstoppable force. . . .

Griffith shut his eyes and focused on his breathing, drawing longer breaths through his nose and exhaling them slowly through his mouth, like his mother had taught him. Feelings of panic were not new to Griffith. They used to happen regularly. Especially when he was younger.

"Are you okay?" Ruby rested her hand on her brother's shoulder.

Griffith nodded and opened his eyes. He tilted the paper so that Ruby could read it too.

He had been so stunned by Uncle Owen's warning that he hadn't even thought to turn the letter over and look for more. It was almost as if the words were hiding, trying not to be discovered. Or at least not by everyone. There was something about the handwriting, too. There was no doubt it was Uncle's Owen's, but at the same time, it seemed different.

"How would the Chancellor find out about the baseball?" Ruby asked, running her fingertips over her pocket to reassure herself that the ball was safe.

Griffith wiped the perspiration from his face with his sleeve but didn't reply.

"Does Uncle Owen think he's watching us?" she pressed.

"I'm not sure." The thrum of the ship's

engines beat louder in Griffith's head. Were they being followed? Was there a link between the Chancellor and their baseball?

Ruby gestured at the letter, then glanced back toward the door. "What do we tell Graham?"

"We don't."

"But he knows a letter arrived."

"This is Grammy we're talking about. All he thinks about is playing baseball. If we don't mention it, he'll just forget about it."

Ruby nodded. "Listen, I'm heading up on deck. It's too hot in here, and I need to get this into my journal. There's a lot I want to write down."

"I'll head up with you." Griffith picked up his glove. "I promised Grammy we'd have a catch."

riffith leaped as high as he could for the baseball, and some-how, it stuck in his leather. "Ease up on those throws, Grambo," he said.

"What are you talking about?" Graham replied. "That throw was perfect!"

LEATHER:
baseball glove or mitt.

"We don't want the crew getting angry with us, and this is the last one we have." Griffith tossed the ball back to his younger brother. "If it ends up in the river, we're going to have to find something else to do for the rest of this trip."

"Then don't drop any more."

"It's not a question of me dropping any more." Griffith leaped for his brother's next high throw, but this one sailed way over his head. "Grammy, what the hay? Who's over *there*?"

Luckily, the ball didn't land in the Ohio River like so many of Graham's other over-throws had. It caromed off a crate and scooted down the deck of the *Meriwether Lewis*.

Graham peeked back down the deck to where their mother was *pretending* not to watch them as she folded clothes. Even though they weren't supposed to be running around, she hadn't minded so long as they stayed away from the edges and didn't disturb the other passengers.

"I'll get it!" Graham charged after the ball.

Griffith shook his head. If he didn't know better, Griffith would have thought Graham

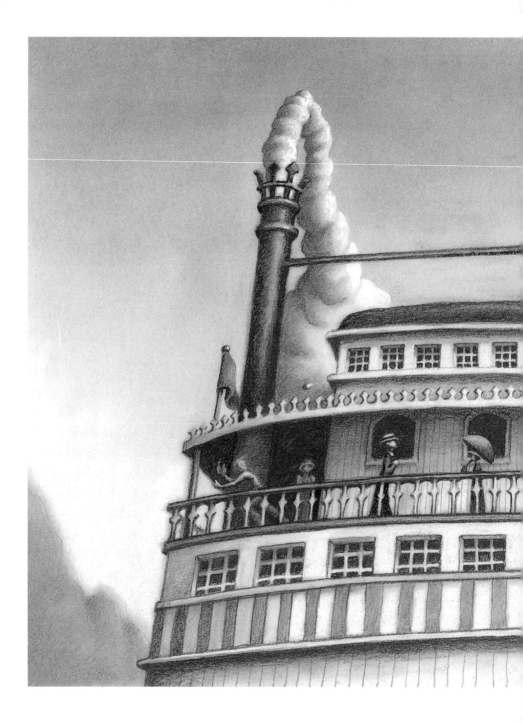

"Ease up on those throws, Grambo."

was *intentionally* throwing wildly just so he could run around the deck. But Graham wasn't doing it on purpose. Whenever and wherever Graham played catch—in their backyard at home, during practices with the barnstormers, or now on the deck of this steamer—he always let loose.

As Graham raced by, he playfully punched his older brother before speeding past and around the bow.

BARNSTORMERS: *team that tours an area playing exhibition games for moneymaking entertainment.*

RAWHIDE: *baseball. Also called "rock" or "pill" (see page 107).*

"You looking for this?" Ruby held up the ball, which had rolled to a stop by her feet. She had been sitting on a crate and writing.

Graham clapped for the rawhide. "Thanks, sis."

"How much is it worth to you?" Ruby teased her younger brother, tossing the ball to herself.

"C'mon, Ruby." Graham clapped again.

"Why don't you practice *aiming* for a change?" She flipped the ball to him. "I moved all the way over here because I was afraid one of your throws would clock me in the noggin!"

"You have nothing to worry about, sis."

"Well, I may not, but what about the poor fishes?"

Ruby wrote furiously in her journal, but her pen couldn't keep up with her brain. Each time she had one thought, three more popped into her head, and the conversation she'd just finishing having with Scribe, the team's center scout, only made them come faster.

"Why weren't you afraid?" Ruby had asked.

"Afraid of what?" Scribe had replied.

She had eyed him sideways. "Of all the strange things that took place during the

SCOUT: *outfielder. The right fielder was called the "right scout," the center fielder was called the "center scout," and the left fielder was called the "left scout."*

13

game in Cincinnati—the fog, the switching signal, the train. Why weren't any of the Travelin' Nine afraid?"

Scribe had smiled his soft smile. "There was no need. After what we experienced during the war, we all knew there was nothing to fear."

"You've never told me those things. What really happened in Cuba?"

"I've told you many tales from the war." He reached down and placed his giant hand on her journal. "Keep writing."

The journal had been a gift from Scribe. He had given it to her at the train depot before the start of their journey back in Washington, D.C. Long ago, before the accident, Ruby's father had told him how she loved to write stories and record her memories.

So far, Ruby had been so busy, all she had written were a few brief entries.

But now, as they headed to Louisville,

Ruby finally had time to reflect, and she was determined to write about as much as she could.

She *needed* to get it *all* down.

My Journal
by Ruby Payne

I'm going to write in my journal every day now. Just like Scribe said I should. He says that's what a good writer does—writes at least a little bit every day. Not only is Scribe the best center fielder I've ever seen, but he's also the best writer. He keeps a journal too. He never lets me read what he writes, but sometimes he'll read some of his entries to me. They always sound like poetry. One day, I'm going to write as well as he does.

<u>The Night of Daddy's Funeral</u>

What Uncle Owen said in his backyard.

– – – – – –→

"Be together. Always."
"Great danger lies ahead.
An unspeakable kind."
"Things will speak to you.
In different ways."
"You mustn't tell a soul.
No one can know of this."

By "this," he meant the baseball.
Some of the things were said to all
of us, but some were only said to Griff.
He's finally told me everything Uncle
Owen told him last month. Griff said he
won't keep secrets from me anymore.
I'm glad he realizes how important it
is for us to work together. I know that's
what Uncle Owen meant.

<u>Uncle Owen's Letter</u>
It has frightened and worried us. What
happened to it? What happened to Uncle Owen?

"Beware the Chancellor"

"He mustn't learn of the baseball"

What is it about the baseball that has Uncle Owen so concerned?

<u>Grammy's Baseball</u>
At the start of each game, we all touch it. It's our pregame ritual. We're not sure why we do that, but it feels right.

The baseball is the connection. It's the link to the strange things that took place on the field in Cincinnati. Griff and I talked about it after the game. We know it is. It has to be.

Still, what caused the strange events to happen? How could we have used them to help the Travelin' Nine? Were they meant to help?

Can we make things happen?

I know this sounds odd, but I keep

thinking about Mom baking her pies and cookies during the holidays and when we have company. She always uses her book of recipes, she carefully chooses the ingredients, and the result is something magical. Somehow I think that Griff, Graham, and I have those ingredients. All of them.

Barnstorming.

* Traveling around from city to city playing exhibition baseball
* To raise money
* Why the Rough Riders have formed the Travelin' Nine

Travelin' Nine = Rough Riders

Professor Lance	Tales
Crazy Feet	Scribe
Woody	Happy
Bubbles	Mom (Guy)
Doc Lindy	

<u>The Game in Cincinnati</u>

Final Score:

Cincinnati Swine 12

Travelin' Nine 3

$$$$$: We didn't earn a single penny. The Swine won all the money.

$\boxed{\text{Over \$700!}}$

<u>Facts About the Game</u>

- ⚾ Some very strange things happened
- ⚾ Only WE could see them
- ⚾ We = Travelin' Nine + ~~Griffith~~ + me + ~~Graham~~
- ⚾ The train signal—rising from the ground all over the field
- ⚾ The fog, the tracks, and the ghost train appearing in different places
- ⚾ The Travelin' Nine weren't afraid because of what happened during the war

<u>Questions About the Game</u>
* Why couldn't the locals see the strange
  things on the field?
* The Travelin' Nine weren't afraid—
  what happened in Cuba?
* Why were Griff, Grammy, and I able
  to see these things too?

I miss Daddy.
So do Griff and Grammy, but Griff will
never admit it or show it. Griff is just
like Daddy. He reminds me of him more
and more every single day.

All of the Travelin' Nine miss Daddy.
They're always talking about him.
Sometimes it hurts to hear them, but at
the same time, it's comforting to know
that everyone loves him and thinks
about him like I do.

★ UNABLE TO SLEEP ★

riffith stood along the railing and stared into the darkness. The half moon, perched in the sky just above the treetops, offered the night's only light.

He couldn't sleep. His mind wouldn't let him. He hadn't slept a single night through since the day their father had died. That was over a month ago. Now Uncle's Owen's letter and losing the game in Cincinnati and not raising any money only made matters worse. Much worse.

Though he would have preferred sleep, Griffith didn't mind being on the deck. He found it peaceful, calming. During the day, he had stood for hours along the rail, fascinated by the changing landscape. At night, with the soft, comfortable breezes blowing, he searched for the forms of that same landscape.

As he strolled toward the stern, Griffith wished he had paper so he could draw. He hadn't done any drawings since the start of the trip west, and sometimes when he couldn't sleep, drawing helped. He thought about asking Ruby for a few sheets from her journal, but he didn't want to wake her, and he knew better than to take without asking.

At the end of the deck, Griffith closed his eyes and listened to the enormous paddles splashing the waters. The constant chugging and churning made it seem as though the boat were traveling in slow motion. He

Griffith closed his eyes.

leaned over the rail, and refreshing mist cooled his face.

Griffith inhaled a long breath. Traveling by steamboat meant he didn't have to be on a train. He hated traveling by train. In the days and weeks ahead, he knew he would be spending countless hours riding the rails, but he hadn't the foggiest idea how he was going to get used to it.

Tracing his hand along the railing, he wandered back up the deck. His thoughts turned to Graham earlier in the day, running around on the steamer. He couldn't help but smile.

"Kentucky!" Graham would call, pointing to the land off the port side of the boat. Then he would race around to the starboard side and cry, "Ohio!" Later in the day, farther down the Ohio River, Graham's cries became "Kentucky!" and "Indiana!"

At the spot where they had played catch,

Griffith stopped. He was constantly amazed at how good his younger brother had become at baseball. Had there ever been a seven-year-old with such a strong throwing arm? It was far more powerful than his own. Still, Graham had a long way to go before he knew how to use all of his talents.

Now when it came to *knowing* the game, it was a completely different story. Graham couldn't compete with Griffith's knowledge of America's new national pastime. But then again, neither could any of the Travelin' Nine.

"Grammy," Griffith liked to remind his brother, "you might be able to hit farther than me and throw harder than me, but let me tell you, I've *forgotten* more about baseball in my eleven years of living than you'll learn in a lifetime!"

Their father used to roar with delight whenever Griffith said that. Griffith missed that laugh, that approving bellow that seemed to hold words and tales of its own.

Griffith sighed. He missed everything about his father. There was so much he still *needed* to ask him and tell him. Griffith had thought there would be time, especially after he had returned home safely from the war.

But then the accident had happened. So out of nowhere. It didn't make any sense. How could their father survive a brutal war, but not a trip across Chesapeake Bay? He had taken that trip hundreds of times with Uncle Owen. What had happened to them out there? What had—

Griffith gasped, then froze.

He couldn't believe his eyes. Even in the dark, he knew exactly what it was the instant he saw it, but it took his brain a few extra moments to acknowledge it was real. Perched atop the railing, only feet from where he stood, was an enormous bald eagle.

He couldn't believe his eyes.

Where did it come from? How long had it been there?

Griffith had never been this near a bald eagle. It was so close that if he were able to move, he could reach over and touch the talons that clutched the railing. Its snow-white neck and hooked orange beak glowed in the moonlight reflecting off the waters. Overlapping layers of feathers covered its breast, feathers that separated at the tips of its wings.

The bird looked up and fixed its gaze on Griffith.

Griffith remained frozen.

That's when the eagle *nodded* at Griffith.

And that's when *the* memory returned, the one from that day many years ago when an eagle had stolen baby Graham from in front of his eyes, the day Griffith thought he had lost his little brother forever. It was his fault; Griffith had never stopped believing that. He could've prevented the horrible ordeal from ever happening.

Griffith blinked hard, shutting the memory away.

When Griffith reopened his eyes, the eagle nodded again. Griffith managed the slightest of nods in return.

With that, the bald eagle spread its wings and leaped from the railing. It soared toward the heavens and disappeared into the night.

★ ON THE STREETS OF LOUISVILLE ★

elcome to Louisville," Professor Lance announced at the corner of Market Street, "the largest city in the great state of Kentucky." He took a deep breath and let go of Graham's hand.

"It's about time!" Graham shook out his arm. He had been itching to be free of the Professor's grasp from the moment they had left the hostel.

"The locals pronounce it *Loo-uh-vul* or just *Loo-vul*," Professor Lance added. He pointed the group down the bustling block. "But either way, they can spot out-of-towners the moment they open their mouths." He eyeballed Graham. "So you, young man, behave yourself. None of that stuff you pulled back in Cincinnati, you hear?"

"I always behave!" Graham declared.

"Beaver dam, Grammy!" Griffith exclaimed. "I do!"

Ruby laughed. "I guess we have different definitions of the word *behave.*"

Griffith turned to his sister. "It's about time you got your nose out of your journal and said something."

Ruby flipped her hair. "I'm writing down everything. We may have missed something back in Cincinnati, and I'm not about to let that happen again."

"Well, you're definitely going to miss something if you're so busy writing you don't even look up," Griffith replied. "And we could sure use your help with Grammy. We have to make sure he—"

"I always behave!" Graham repeated, shaking his hands at the group. "Now, c'mon!" He waved everyone forward. "Time to round up some cranks!"

As they turned off Market and headed down Sixth Street, Ruby wrote as feverishly as ever. Every few steps she would stop, jot down what she saw or something Tales said, and then race to catch up with the others.

CRANKS: *fans, usually the hometown fans. Also called "rooters" (see page 58).*

Tales had joined the group for the trip into Louisville just as Bubbles had in Cincinnati. Since the Travelin' Nine's second baseman was from here, Professor Lance had thought it would be helpful if he showed them around. Professor Lance also knew he wouldn't have to worry about Tales wanting to share every last piece of information about his hometown like Bubbles had back in Porkopolis.

That's not to say Tales wasn't talkative.

He most certainly was. In fact, Ruby often heard his teammates refer to him as "the talking mustache"! But unlike Bubbles, Tales saved his yapping for the playing field. Between the white lines, Tales was constant chatter—scouting the strikers, positioning his players, and even providing the play-by-play as the action unfolded.

BETWEEN THE WHITE LINES: *on the playing field, in fair territory.*

SCOUTING: *observing and evaluating players on the opposing side.*

STRIKERS: *batters or hitters.*

"Do you know what they call Loo-vul?" Tales asked at the next corner.

"The River City!" Graham boomed. "There was a sign at the pier."

"Indeed!" Professor Lance replied.

Graham spun back toward the river. Over the rooftops, he could still see the tall stacks of the steamboats lining the harbor. He even recognized the red, white, and blue–painted stacks of the *Meriwether Lewis.*

"Which way now, Mr. President?" Griffith asked Tales.

Graham looked to his brother. "Why do you call him that?"

"Because his real name is Zachary Taylor," Griffith replied, "and that happens to be the name of the former President of the United States, raised right near Louisville."

Tales tapped his wire-rimmed spectacles and twitched his bushy mustache. Then he took the oversized and overflowing satchel of fliers from the Professor and pointed up the street in the direction of a row of brick Victorian mansions with stained glass windows.

Griffith glanced back to Ruby still standing and writing at the corner. "Are you taking notes or writing a book?" he asked.

"Tease me all you want," Ruby replied, trotting back over. "You'll be thanking me later. You'll see."

Even with Ruby next to him, Griffith still stared at the spot where she had been standing. He could have sworn there had been a man in a suit directly behind her, looking over her shoulder. When Griffith had turned, the man had slipped into the entranceway of the shoe repair shop on the corner.

"What are you looking at?" Ruby asked.

"I thought . . . ," Griffith stammered, "I thought I saw someone. I guess I was mistaken."

"If you say so."

BASE BALL! BASE BALL! BASE·BALL!

August 12, 1899, at Cherokee Park

A SENSATIONAL SATURDAY WITH YOUR SUMMER SLUGGERS.

Come see Rube Waddell, Pete Browning, "Bud" Hillerich, & the REST of the River City's FINEST NINE

take on America's HEROES,

Roosevelt's Rough Riders

★ THE RIVER CITY SHOWDOWN ★

nce they crossed Ormsby Avenue and reached the entrance to Central Park, it was time to get down to business.

Ruby reached over and tucked her journal into the side compartment of the satchel slung over Tales's shoulder. Then she removed a batch of fliers for herself and a stack for both Griffith and Graham. But before handing his to Graham, she offered a few words.

"Do us all a favor," she said, "please don't start any fights this time." She winked at him.

"I didn't pick any fights." Graham smiled

mischievously. "They started with me."

"You're right." Ruby smiled because she knew just how effective his *feisty* approach had been. "Go do your thing!"

"You might make the best bats in the whole wide world," Graham taunted an older boy, "but the Travelin' Nine can beat you with broomsticks!"

While listening to Tales, Graham had learned that Louisville was the home of J.F. Hillerich & Son, makers of the Louisville Slugger, the most feared timber in all of baseball. Now, he was attempting to use that new knowledge to his advantage.

"You might make the best bats in the whole wide world," Graham said as he turned and faced an older girl, "but the Travelin' Nine can beat you with saw mill slats!"

"You think you can beat the Louisville Summer Sluggers?" The girl laughed,

TIMBER: *baseball bat. Also known as "lumber"* (*see page 70*).

snatching a flier from Graham. "Obviously, you're not from these parts."

Graham grinned as his latest target played right into his hands. "Obviously, you haven't seen the Travelin' Nine play," he said.

"Don't need to." She pointed down at Graham. "You think you stand a chance against Rube Waddell? Do you know what we call him?" She crumpled the flier into a ball. "The Louisville Lightning!"

Graham inflated his chest. "By the time the Travelin' Nine get through with Ruby *Waddles* or whatever his name is, the Louisville Lightning will be the Louisville Loser!"

The older girl fired the balled-up paper at Graham, hitting him square in the nose.

Graham growled like a grizzly and lunged at her, smacking the hat from her head.

"Now you've done it!" The older girl kicked at Graham's foot, but Graham shuffled away.

She drew back her fist.

"You missed," Graham goaded. "You're too slow."

The girl shook out her hat and slapped it on her head. Then she drew back her fist and swung, but Graham bobbed out of the way.

"You can't touch me. I float like a butterfly!"

The girl swung with her other fist, but Graham ducked below the roundhouse.

"Not even close!" Graham stuck out his chin and baited her to take another shot.

This time, the girl clenched both fists, but instead of taking another swing, she stomped a foot and stormed away.

"Grammy!" Griffith charged over. "You promised."

"I was behaving!" Graham smacked his own leg. "She started it!"

"It doesn't matter," Griffith replied. "You can't go around picking fights."

"But she started it," Graham still insisted.

"Griff, I saw the whole thing," Ruby chimed in. "She picked on him. Grammy was defending his—"

Professor Lance stepped between the squabbling siblings. "I for one feel we have to be friendly at all times. We're guests here." He adjusted the cord of the eye patch that covered his left eye. "Nevertheless, we did accomplish what we set out to do."

"We sure did!" Tales patted the empty satchel. "I didn't think there was any chance we'd get through this entire bag. I am mighty impressed! You three are naturals."

Graham looked at his sister and brother and smiled. "We do make a pretty good team, don't we?" he said.

"We sure do, Grams!" Ruby patted her

brother's shoulder. "Mission accomplished!"

"We worked together," Graham added. "Like Uncle Owen said we should."

"Indeed!" Professor Lance declared. "Now before we head back to the hostel, we have one more stop to make. It's a real quick ride from here."

And just as he had in Cincinnati, Professor Lance steered the group onto a trolley heading toward their destination.

While the others managed to find seats toward the front of the crowded streetcar, Graham opted to stand for the short ride. At first, he twirled around one of the poles in the center aisle, but the Professor made him stop after he knocked into another passenger. So instead, he leaned out a window cutout as the car clanked up the block. When he spotted the racetrack's spires up ahead, Graham drew his head back in.

That's when he saw the old man, through the passengers. He stood by himself in the doorway at the back of the car.

He was dirty and disheveled. His shirt hung in ragged tatters, and his trousers were stiff with grime. He wasn't wearing any shoes, either; his bare feet were caked with earth. And his unkempt gray and white beard reached all the way down to his chest.

But the old man's most startling trait was his eyes. Even from the opposite end of the trolley, Graham could see that behind those round, wire-rimmed glasses were eyes of *different* colors. One was clouded over and milky white, while the other twinkled a most brilliant bright blue.

For a moment, Graham wondered if the old man was even real. He seemed more like an apparition, a ghost. Graham turned

47

He seemed . . . like an apparition.

to Ruby and Griffith, seated next to Tales. Griffith was staring at the city sights; Ruby was writing. Neither was aware of the man at the back of the trolley.

Graham reached over to tap his sister at the same moment the old man looked up. He fixed his gaze on Graham and nodded.

Graham couldn't move.

The old man nodded again, and only then could Graham manage the slightest of nods in return.

"Our stop!" Tales announced.

Startled by the voice, Graham jumped. How long had he and the man been standing there, staring?

"Are you okay, Grammy?" Ruby asked.

"Something the matter?" Griffith draped an arm around his brother. "You look like you've seen a ghost."

Graham glanced toward the back of the car, but a crowd of new passengers blocked his view. He could no longer see the old man, except for his bare feet.

"I'm fine," Graham said.

Then he leaped over the railing and off the trolley.

★ CHURCHILL DOWNS ★

o trip to Louisville is complete without a visit to Churchill Downs," Professor Lance said. "Your father would've insisted."

"I can understand why," Ruby said, staring in awe.

"Home of the Kentucky Derby," Tales declared, "the crown jewel of horse racing."

"I wish all the Travelin' Nine could see this," Professor Lance said.

"Huzzah!" Tales declared.

"But they needed to practice today," the

"HUZZAH!": *common cheer to show appreciation for a team's efforts.*

"I wish all the Travelin' Nine could see this."

Professor added, "and that's quite under-standable given the outcome of our first game. Hopefully, they'll get here before we head out of town."

Tales nodded. "The Rough Riders would never want to leave."

"I don't want to leave," Griffith said.

"Me neither," agreed Graham.

All five gaped at the racetrack: the cobble-stone streets leading in; the row of stables in the distance; the tiered grandstand with its twin spires piercing the summer sky; the enormous oval; and, most stunning of all, the array of flowers and trees in all their splendor.

Ruby peered up at the sign affixed to the grandstand. In order of finish, it listed all the wonderful and unusual names of the horses that had run in the Kentucky Derby in the 1890s. Some were so quirky and odd they caused her to giggle out loud. The name at the top of each column—the year's winning horse—appeared in bright red. There was even a column underneath the year 1900, waiting to be filled in next May.

Without thinking, Ruby slid her hand into her side pocket and placed it atop the baseball. She traced her fingers over the lacing and inserted her pinky into the odd, acorn-size hole.

Suddenly, the baseball shuddered.

And during that briefest of instances, the words *Lieutenant Gibson* appeared in bright red in that empty space atop the column underneath the year 1900.

But Ruby knew that couldn't be possible.

Could it?

She pulled her pencil from her pocket, flipped open her journal, and began writing as fast as she could.

The Dragon. Parson. Lieber Karl. The Winner. Isabey.

"What are you doing?" Griffith asked.

"Taking good notes," she replied without looking up. "I need to write down all of the names."

"All?"

"Yes, all."

"Need?" Graham asked.

"Yes." Ruby still didn't look up.

"Why?" her brothers asked together.

Ruby didn't know why. She just knew that she did.

★ STUNNED DISBELIEF ★

entlemen, this is a contest of speed," the umpire explained, holding his top hat over his chest. "The first good man around these bases decides which team is the home team."

Ruby sized up the runners standing by home plate and preparing for their dash around the diamond. She smiled confidently. There was no doubt in her mind that Crazy Feet was going to win.

She shielded her eyes from the sun. While it was still plenty warm, it wasn't nearly as hot as it had been in Cincinnati, and the fair-weather clouds provided relief from the heat.

Ruby turned around and faced the swelling throngs. More and more people kept coming and coming! The pregame festivities had been scheduled for high noon, but the game wasn't beginning until half past two because it had taken *that* long to clear the field of spectators. In fact, so many had shown up that some of the events had to be scrapped.

But not the traditional pregame foot race.

For the Louisville Summer Sluggers, Rube Waddell had stepped forth, and the moment he set foot on the field, Ruby could hardly believe her ears and eyes. The crowd flew into a frenzy, especially those crammed into "Rube's Rooters' Row," the hometown hurler's very own cheering section.

"My good man," the umpire motioned

ROOTERS: *fans; people who cheer at ball games. Also called "cranks" (see page 34).*

HURLER: *pitcher.*

to Rube Waddell, "you will be running the bases in the conventional direction." He pointed toward first base.

"Ready!" Rube Waddell replied.

The umpire turned to Crazy Feet. "My good man, you will be running the bases in the reverse direction." He pointed toward third base.

Crazy Feet nodded his response since he was never a man of many words (or *any* words for that matter).

"*Go!*"

The sudden start caught Crazy Feet off guard, but he still broke evenly with his adversary. The crowd roared as the two men rounded their first turns. Then down the backstretches they raced, crisscrossing at second bag and barely avoiding a head-on collision. As they reached their far turns, the two remained neck-and-neck.

A wide-eyed Ruby held her breath.

BAG: *base, as in "second bag." Also called "sack" (see page 87).*

59

A last, sudden burst

"Down the stretch they come!" the umpire cried as if he were calling a race at Churchill Downs. He positioned himself behind the dish and fixed his eyes on the finish as both speedsters raced for home.

Ruby clenched her teeth and fists.

With a last, sudden burst, Rube Waddell crossed the plate a length before Crazy Feet. The already crazed crowd erupted like a volcano as Waddell danced in circles before taking a victory lap around the diamond.

DISH: *home plate.*

Ruby's mouth fell open.

Crazy Feet had *lost.*

Griffith clasped his hands behind his head. His mouth dropped wide open. He couldn't believe what he had just witnessed.

Neither could the Travelin' Nine. They stood in stunned disbelief as Crazy Feet returned to the team's bench behind third base. No one had ever seen him lose a foot race. No one had even thought it was possible for Crazy Feet to lose a foot race.

But he just had.

Griffith's mind began to churn. How could the fastest man *any* of the Travelin' Nine had ever known lose? Something had to be wrong.

He turned to Ruby, his eyes drawn to the ball in her pocket. Maybe they should have been holding it prior to the race. Could that have been the reason Crazy Feet had lost?

"I need to be alone for a minute," Griffith said, stepping to his sister.

"What is it?" she asked.

Griffith shook his head. "I'm fine. Honest. Just wait here. I promise I'll be right back."

Griffith needed to figure out a plan, a strategy for using their baseball during the game. All he needed was a moment or two to get his mind focused.

But as he walked through the cranks

gathering beyond the left garden foul line, he spotted a man helping another man out of a wheelchair. Griffith stopped. He wondered if they were brothers.

In a flash, Griffith's thoughts leaped to his father. Not to how much he missed him, as was so often the case these days. But rather, this time, Griffith recalled a *specific* memory.

In his head, Griffith heard his father's voice explaining the reasons he needed to go off to fight in the war against Spain last year. Like all Americans, Guy had been enraged by the sinking of the USS *Maine* in Havana harbor and the killing of two hundred and sixty United States servicemen. Guy believed his love of country required him to defend and protect his nation's honor.

And then, when he had learned that among the dead was the entire Navy baseball team, the champions of the U.S. military,

LEFT GARDEN:
left field. The outfield was once known as the garden. So center field was referred to as "center garden" and right field was called "right garden."

FOUL LINES:
lines extending from home plate through first and third base and all the way to the outfield. Anything within the lines is considered to be in fair territory; anything outside the lines is in foul territory.

Guy had realized his service was a calling. Some of the best and brightest young stars in all of baseball had perished. Only one player had survived, along with the team's mascot, a goat.

That conversation had taken place at the wooden table in Uncle Owen's backyard.

"I'll be joining you," Uncle Owen had said to their father. "I need to look out for my older brother."

Griffith recalled his father's expression of surprise upon hearing Uncle's Owen's declaration. Clearly, he hadn't expected his brother to come with him. Or such a showing of brotherly love. His father had turned away in order to hide his tears.

Griffith rubbed his eyes and looked back at Ruby and Graham. His heart skipped a beat. A man in a freshly pressed suit stood only yards away from their location by the players' bench. Was he staring at them?

Griffith took one step in their direction, and that's when the man looked his way. They locked eyes momentarily, and then the man disappeared into the cranks.

Drawing in a deep breath and letting it out slowly, Griffith resolved to keep his guard up. At all times. Because he needed to protect his mother, Ruby, and Graham.

He especially needed to look out for Graham. He still wasn't quite sure why; he only knew that he did.

"You coming back?"

Griffith gasped.

Ruby had walked over. She laughed. "Someone's a little jumpy."

"Where's Grams?"

"Relax," Ruby replied. "He's with Lindy on the bench."

Griffith patted his chest as he exhaled.

"What are you thinking about?" she asked.

"Nothing," he said.

"Nothing? Griffith Payne, when are you not thinking about something? You're always thinking."

Griffith managed a smile.

"So are you going to tell me?" she pressed.

"A lot of things. Too many."

"What are you thinking right now?"

Griffith glanced over at his little brother. He was standing beside Happy and Doc, tossing a ball into the air and attempting to catch it under his leg. Like he didn't have a care in the world. And at that moment, Griffith felt the same way he had after the game in Cincinnati.

"This has to do with Graham." Griffith turned back to his sister.

"What does?" she asked.

"Everything. Dad, the money, the stuff in Cincinnati, the unspeakable danger. Everything."

"What makes you say that?"

Griffith shrugged. "Just a feeling. One I've been getting more and more."

"Me too."

"Seriously?"

Ruby nodded. "I'm sure of it."

"We need to protect him, Ruby."

"I know." She touched her brother's arm. "And we are."

Griffith peered at the players warming up on the field. "I feel like we need to be doing even more."

"Like what, Griff? We're together, we're learning things, we're looking out for one another, and I for one believe that things are going to work out. That's how we're helping the Travelin' Nine. And that's how we're protecting Grammy."

"Our baseball will help too," Griffith added.

"We all should hold on to it more during the game."

Griffith nodded. "I wish I had a better feeling about today's game," he said, looking across the diamond and sizing up the Louisville Nine.

"I have a great feeling." She pointed at Griffith. "And so should you."

Griffith felt his frown. The Rough Riders may have been skilled sportsmen, but the Louisville Nine were skilled *ballists*. Some even looked like professionals! And for good reason. Since the Louisville Colonels, the city's official team, had the day off, they'd lent the Summer Sluggers a few key players. So some of their ballists *were* professionals!

Griffith couldn't spot a weak link anywhere in their lineup. In addition to Rube Waddell, the Summer Sluggers also had John A. "Bud" Hillerich, the founder and president of the famous bat-making operation. "Mr. Louisville Slugger" batted cleanup, but his lumber wasn't even close to being the most potent in the lineup. That bat belonged to the fellow who followed him in the order, Pete Browning. This hulking left fielder was *the* force to be reckoned with when he was grasping the timber. And then over at first base—

"Striker to the line!"

BALLISTS: *players.*

CLEANUP: *the batter who bats fourth in the lineup.*

LUMBER: *baseball bat. Also called "timber" (see page 41).*

"STRIKER TO THE LINE!": *what the umpire announced at the start of each contest. It was also called out at each batter's turn. Today the umpire yells, "Batter up!"*

"I wish I had a better feeling about today's game."

★ THE GAME BEGINS ★

s if the umpire's call was her cue, Ruby removed the base-ball from her side pocket and placed it in Griffith's open hand. Then she hurried over to Graham, still standing by the players' bench, and walked him down the left field line to Griffith.

It was time.

They stood among the cranks, but none in the crowd were paying attention to them. All eyes were fixed on the field.

Griffith held the baseball out to his

brother and sister, and just like they had before the game in Cincinnati, all three joined hands on it.

"Here we go," Ruby said.

"Start us off!" Griffith called as Crazy Feet stepped to the plate.

Crazy Feet was the ideal leadoff batter. Not only could he run like the wind, but he could hit to all fields, work out a walk, and even provide some thunder at the top of the lineup.

THUNDER: *power.*
Also called "pop"
(see page 159).

"C'mon, Crazy Feet!" Graham cheered nervously.

Rube Waddell's first pitch was a fastball, but a fastball unlike any they had ever seen. The ball moved! As it blazed a path toward the plate, it fluttered from side to side.

Crazy Feet tried to check his confused swing, but he couldn't, popping up meekly to the pitcher.

All three joined hands on it.

The moment the ball landed in the Louisville Lightning's leather, he leaped off the mound and clicked his heels. He danced in circles as all the cranks—especially those crammed into Rube's Rooters' Row—hooted and hollered.

One hand down.

"C'mon, Tales!" Ruby cheered as the Travelin' Nine's second sack man stepped to the plate.

Graham lifted his hand off the baseball and stepped in front of his brother and sister.

"Where are you going?" Griffith asked.

"I want to get a better view," Graham answered.

"We all should have a hand on the baseball," Ruby said.

"That didn't help Crazy Feet." Graham gestured to the Travelin' Nine's left scout.

At the dish, Tales dug in. He flapped his

HAND DOWN: *an out. ONE HAND DOWN meant "one out," TWO HANDS DOWN meant "two outs," and THREE HANDS DOWN (or DEAD) meant "three outs."*

SECOND SACK MAN: *second baseman. The first baseman was often called the "first sack man" and the third baseman was often called the "third sack man."*

elbow four times, but fared no better. He grounded out with a hit that would have barely bruised a bug.

Two hands down.

"They're not looking too good." Graham peered up at his brother and sister.

Griffith nodded. He looked at the baseball in his hands and then back at his brother. Had Graham let go of the ball too soon? Ruby was right; they all should hold on to the ball longer. Perhaps that was the reason things weren't going well for the Travelin' Nine.

"It's only the top of the first," Ruby replied. "The Rough Riders aren't even loose yet. They're still warming up."

"I hope you're right." Graham looked to the diamond again. "C'mon, Woody!" he cheered as the barnstormers' right scout stepped to the line.

Not only did Woody have a reliable

STEP TO THE LINE (V.): *to prepare to hit.*

glove and the strongest outfield arm on the squad, but he was also a specialist with the lumber. All of the Travelin' Nine knew Woody was the best all-around striker on the team.

But against the Louisville Lightning, Woody fared even worse than Crazy Feet and Tales (if that was possible).

Fastball. Strike one.

Fastball. Strike two.

Fastball. Strike three!

Three hands dead. In the blink of an eye, the inning was over.

In the bottom of the first, the Louisville Summer Sluggers struck fast and frequently. By the end of the opening frame, the barnstormers already trailed by three tallies.

As Scribe stepped to the dish to start the second, Griffith pulled Graham closer.

FRAME: *inning.*

TALLIES: *runs scored. On some fields, whenever the home team scored, a tally bell would sound. The tally keeper was the official scorer or scorekeeper. A tally was also known as an "ace."*

77

"Stand back over here with us," he said to his younger brother. "Let's all hold the ball again. Maybe that will help turn things around."

But even with all three Paynes touching their baseball, the Travelin' Nine's fortunes didn't exactly improve in that second frame.

Neither Griffith nor his brother or sister spoke a sentence or moved a muscle when Scribe grounded to first, Professor Lance popped to third, and Doc Linden stuck out. And neither Griffith nor his brother or sister spoke a sentence or moved a muscle when the Louisville Nine tacked on two more tallies to the three they had recorded in the first.

"They're getting destroyed!" Graham exclaimed.

"It's only been two innings," Ruby said, tucking the ball back into her pocket.

"There's plenty of baseball left to be played," Griffith added.

But as much as Griffith wanted to believe that, he couldn't help but share some of his brother's doubts.

1	2	3	4	5	6	7	8	9	R
TN 55	0 3	0 2							0 5

10

★ THE RUBE WADDELL SHOW ★

hey're called the Travelin' Nine," Rube Waddell said, strutting to the mound to start the third frame. "But I don't need nine players. Watch me beat them with only *two*!"

"What does that mean?" Graham asked.

Ruby bit her lower lip. "I have a bad feeling about this."

"You and me both." Griffith sighed. "You and me both."

Ruby pointed to the pitcher. "That hurler is one crafty southpaw. This might not be pretty."

SOUTHPAW: a left-handed individual. The commonly used nickname for players who throw left-handed.

With a large amount of fanfare, the Louisville Lightning waved his teammates *off* the field. And as they trotted to their bench, the cranks erupted. The men tossed their hats, the ladies twirled their parasols, and the children danced in circles.

"I don't like the looks of this," Ruby said. "Not one bit."

On four pitches, Rube Waddell walked Guy. Then on four more pitches, he walked Bubbles. And on four more, he walked Happy.

"What's he doing?" Graham asked.

"You don't want to know," Ruby answered.

Griffith shook his head. "Daddy wouldn't have appreciated sportsmanship like this."

"I don't either." Ruby folded her arms.

"It has no place in baseball," Griffith added.

"What are you two talking about?" Graham scrunched his face into a knot. "What's he doing?"

"Watch," they answered together.

On the next three pitches, Rube Waddell struck out Crazy Feet, who kicked the dirt in disgust as he retreated to the bench.

"Let's go, boys!" Doc Linden stormed past his teammates. "Let's show a little ginger out here! One swing of the timber puts us right back in this!"

Even from far away, the three Paynes could hear Doc's frustration.

GINGER: *hustle and enthusiasm.*

Up stepped Tales, but he struck out on three straight as well. As Tales walked from the dish, he didn't want the Louisville Lightning to know that he had gotten under his skin. So instead of removing his cap and swatting his leg like he usually did when he was annoyed, he merely twirled the ends of his bushy mustache.

"I reckon someone needs to put a stop to these shenanigans," Woody announced, stepping to the plate.

"But I don't need nine players."

But three pitches later, Woody had struck out.

"Beaver dam!" Graham cried. "We have to do something! It's only the third inning, and we're already losing five to nil."

Graham reached into his sister's pocket, removed the baseball, and shook it in the direction of the tally board behind home plate.

But was that all he did? Because the moment he raised the ball . . .

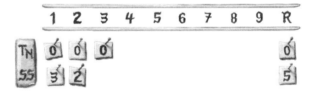

11

★ HORSES, HORSES, EVERYWHERE! ★

t started beyond the trees in right garden, rustling the leaves. At the infield, it turned into a swirling gust, genie-ing up the dust from the dirt-spotted base paths. It whooshed through the masses, turning heads and dropping jaws.

The breeze.

So similar to the one in Cincinnati. Yet so different.

Everyone felt the breeze, players and cranks alike.

Graham reached for his sister. "What did I just do?"

Ruby swallowed. "I don't know if you did that."

"But what if I did?" Graham now held on to Griffith as well. "What did I just do?"

"I think we're about to find out," Griffith whispered.

Ruby looked to the Travelin' Nine taking the field. All seventeen eyes filled with curiosity as they followed the welcome wind. After what they had experienced in Cincinnati, they all knew something was coming. Something was about to happen.

But they had no idea what.

One by one, they began to appear. The first one, chestnut in color with white markings on its hind legs, popped up between Doc Linden and Bubbles. Then a mammoth brown one, with awesomely defined withers, sprang up by Woody. A black one by second sack, a bay one next to Guy, and before long, a half dozen horses grazed the grass, each one more muscled and striking than the next.

Horses, horses, everywhere!

Ruby inched forward. She placed her hand over Graham's, which still clutched the baseball.

Without a doubt, the sudden appearance of the steeds had surprised the barnstormers. Crazy Feet nearly jumped out of his boots when a gray one with a long neck showed up alongside him in left, and Professor Lance stumbled to the turf when a black one with a white stripe down its nose straddled first sack. Of course, each of the ballists backed off whenever a thoroughbred appeared too close because they all knew how flighty and nervous these animals could be.

SACK: *base, as in "first sack." Also called "bag" (see page 59).*

Ruby thought back to what Scribe had told her on the steamboat. She knew why none of the Travelin' Nine seemed scared.

Horses, horses, everywhere!

These horses may not have been expected, but they weren't completely *unexpected* either.

And because the barnstormers weren't afraid, neither was Ruby (or her brothers). Sure she was startled, but after what she had witnessed in Porkopolis, she was more curious than anything else—curious as to whether or not these horses could *help* the Travelin' Nine. Now one horse trotted in a circle around Scribe in center garden, another chewed on the grass near Happy on the hill, and still another pranced about behind Guy at the dish. And just like she had back at Churchill Downs, Ruby giggled out loud at some of the names—Plutus, Boundless, Buck McCann— printed on the saddlecloths.

HILL: *pitcher's mound.*

"Griffy, they can't see the horses," Ruby said, referring to the Louisville Nine, standing atop their bench. "Look at how they're watching the barnstormers."

90

"Their cranks can't see them either," Griffith added. "Take a look at the kids in the crowd. If they could see the horses, they'd be going nuts!"

"It's Cincinnati all over again!" Graham said.

"Exactly." Griffith said.

"They're *ghost* horses!" Graham exclaimed.

"They're beautiful." Ruby took her fingers from the baseball and clasped her hands in front of her.

"What do you think they are going to do?" Graham asked.

"I'm not sure." Griffith shook his head. He looked to Ruby. "Any ideas?"

Ruby pulled out her journal and fanned the pages until she reached the notes she had taken at Churchill Downs. She looked at all the names she had insisted on writing, every single horse that had raced in the Kentucky Derby since the year she was born. On a separate page, she had listed each year's winner, as well as the finishing time, margin of victory, and post position.

"For the time being," Ruby said, looking back out at the field, "let's just watch."

And watch they did!

The arrival of the horses generated a new sense of hope among the Travelin' Nine. On the hill, Happy suddenly seized command of his pitches. He fanned one batter, forced another to sky harmlessly to Scribe, and retired the third on a dribbler to Doc.

FAN (V.): *to strike out.*

SKY (V.): *to hit a fly ball.*

DRIBBLER: *slowly hit ground ball.*

"Whatever they're doing now," Griffith said, "they're doing it right!"

"Whatever *we're* doing," Ruby added, "*we're* doing it right. Let's keep believing that the Travelin' Nine are going to win."

"Go, barnstormers!" Graham cheered.

Things were going better, and the Louisville Nine—as well as their supporters—could sense it too. Even if they couldn't see the ghost horses grazing on the field, the locals could certainly see the improved fortunes of the Travelin' Nine.

As the Travelin' Nine left the pitch at the end of the third inning, so did the horses. But instead of returning with the ballists to the bench, they fell into formation along the first base line and paraded out into right garden. Then they disappeared into the trees beyond the field as if they were retiring to their stables at the end of a long day.

PITCH: *playing field. Also called "green oasis" (see page 107).*

The moment the barnstormers retook their positions in the fourth and fifth frames, the horses materialized from nowhere once again. And when they reappeared, the Travelin' Nine hardly reacted at all.

Like they had in the third, the thoroughbreds on the field lifted the spirits of the barnstormers. All the horses did was graze,

but that seemed to be enough. Their mere presence inspired the Travelin' Nine, especially Happy.

In those fourth and fifth innings, in a dazzling display of pitching perfection, Happy Hoover and Rube Waddell matched each other strike for strike. Unfortunately for the Travelin' Nine, that meant they still hadn't managed a single hit. So far their only base runners remained the ones who had

been intentionally walked by the Louisville
Lightning back in the third.

Griffith snapped his fingers. "I have an
idea."

	1	2	3	4	5	6	7	8	9	R
TN	0	0	0	0	0					0
SS	3	2	0	0	0					5

★LEARNED IN LOUISVILLE★

et's go over what we saw in Louisville," Griffith suggested as the barnstormers bounded back to the bench and the horses faded into the forest.

"Why should we do that?" Graham asked.

Griffith drew his brother and sister closer. "The last few innings, when we've been cheering together and focusing on the game, the Travelin' Nine have been playing much better. But they still haven't been able to make up any ground. We need to be doing more."

"What else can we do?" Graham asked. He massaged the baseball like a hurler stepping to the hill.

"When we all hold the baseball, it seems to help, but not all the time. It's not enough."

"You think what we learned in Louisville could make the difference?" Ruby asked.

Griffith tapped the cover of Ruby's journal. "I think it may."

Ruby smiled. "Aren't you happy I take good notes?'

Griffith didn't respond.

"'Are you taking notes or writing a book?'" Ruby sassed. She teasingly tapped her foot. "I'm waiting for my thank-you."

"Yes, Ruby." Griffith sighed. "I'm glad you take good notes. Thank you."

"That wasn't so difficult, was it?"

"Now can we go over what we learned?" Griffith asked as Crazy Feet stepped to the dish.

All three huddled around Ruby's journal. They read together:

Louisville = The River City

Steamboats of the Ohio River
+ Trains of the Baltimore & Ohio Railway

= Louisville, a bustling metropolis!

"Louisville was founded by George Rogers Clark in 1778," Ruby declared.

"He named the city for King Louis XVI of France," Griffith added, "because the king helped the colonists during the Revolutionary War."

"Kentucky was the fifteenth state!" Graham announced, climbing atop the large boulder behind his brother and sister. "It joined the union in 1792."

Whack!

Huddled around Ruby's journal

Crazy Feet lashed a single to center that buzzed by Rube Waddell's left ear. The Travelin' Nine finally had their first hit.

"Hunky!" Griffith pumped a fist. "We might be onto something. What else did we learn?"

"They call Kentucky the Bluegrass State," Graham answered, "but the grass isn't really blue. In the springtime, when you look at all the buds from a distance, the grass looks purple and blue. That's how it is all over the state, and that's how Kentucky earned its nickname."

HUNKY: *splendid, as in "hunky play."*

"Way to pay attention, Grams!" Griffith applauded.

Whack!

Tales smacked the first pitch he saw from the Louisville Lightning right through the hurler's legs and into center field. The Travelin' Nine had their second hit.

Ruby grew excited. Even without the

100

horses on the field, she and her brothers seemed to be fueling the Travelin' Nine's rally. Was their brainstorming helping the barnstormers?

"Bats!" she suddenly exclaimed. Her eyes were once again glued to her journal. "Listen to this.

"The Louisville Slugger

"Fifteen years ago, young Bud Hillerich, an apprentice in his father's woodshop, made his very first wooden baseball bat. He made it for Pete 'the Old Gladiator' Browning. At the time, the power-hitting Browning was in a horrible slump, so young Hillerich offered to make the local hero a new bat. Swinging his custom-made timber of white

ash, the very first Louisville Slugger, Browning went three-for-three. Almost overnight, everyone wanted their own Louisville Slugger baseball bat, and that was how Hillerich started the most famous baseball bat company in the whole world!"

Ruby motioned to the field. "That's the same Bud Hillerich and Pete Browning playing for the Summer Sluggers right now!"

"Great work, Ruby!" Griffith squeezed his sister's shoulder.

Whack!

Woody stroked a single up the middle that buzzed by Rube Waddell's right ear. The Travelin' Nine had their third hit and the bases loaded.

However, even as the three Paynes continued to read from Ruby's journal and tell one

another what they'd learned, the Louisville
Lightning got Scribe to bounce back to the
hill, forcing Crazy Feet out at the plate. Then
he struck out Professor Lance.

"Beaver dam!" Graham growled, hopping
down from the rock. "Why can't the Travelin'
Nine score?"

"They will," Ruby assured him. "You
gotta believe."

She looked to Griffith. He pinched the bridge of his nose and stared hard at the field. She knew he was thinking exactly what she was. Perhaps the reason the Travelin' Nine had collected back-to-back-to-back singles had nothing to do with their brainstorming. Maybe they were getting these hits and outs on their own.

"Where are the horses?" Graham grumbled. He banged the baseball against his forehead.

"They'll be here," Ruby spoke to the field.

"And why don't they do anything?" Graham continued. "All they do is stand around. How does that help the Travelin' Nine? We need runs!"

Griffith rested his chin in his hand. The Travelin' Nine had finally managed their first hits, but they still hadn't recorded a tally. Trailing by five with the bases loaded, they couldn't afford to come away empty-handed. Graham was right. They *needed* runs.

But Graham had started to walk away.

"Grammy, where are you going?" Griffith asked.

"I don't know," he muttered without turning back.

"Don't go anywhere, Grams," Griffith said to his brother. When Graham didn't stop, Griffith barked. "Get back here!"

Griffith gasped. He rarely—if ever—spoke to his brother with such an edge. But Graham was giving up. Because so many things had gone wrong, Griffith often felt like giving up too. But he couldn't allow any of them to. They had to keep trying. Too much was riding on this game (probably even more than he realized).

Slowly, Graham walked back over to his brother and sister.

"We have to have faith," Ruby said. She placed her hand atop the baseball that Graham still clutched.

"We have to stay strong." Griffith softened his tone. "It's hard sometimes, but we have to."

Graham nodded to his brother. "I'm trying." Then he smiled at his sister. "I do have faith." And as Doc Linden stepped to the plate, he shouted, "Let's go, Lindy!"

With two outs and three ducks on the pond, they were still only one whip of the willow away from being right back in the game.

Griffith clenched a fist and placed his other hand atop his brother's and sister's. "C'mon," he whispered as Doc scowled at the Louisville Lightning rocking into his delivery.

Ruby wove her fingers into Grammy's and slid her pinky into the acorn-sized hole. The moment she did . . .

Horses appeared all over the field!

Crack!

Doc Lindy laced a screamer toward the

THREE DUCKS ON THE POND: *three men on base, i.e., bases loaded. The three ducks refer to the runners; the pond refers to the field.*

WHIP OF THE WILLOW: *swing of the bat.*

SCREAMER: *hard-hit fly ball.*

Summer Sluggers's second sack man. He reached out his leather, but a horse, which had popped up to his right, extended its hind leg and, with the tip of its hoof, punted the pill across the diamond. The redirected rock ricocheted toward short left garden. The short stop charged out, the left scout sped in, but before either could reach the ball, another ghost horse had surfaced and extended its front leg, and with the tip of its hoof, booted the ball back across the green oasis. The right scout raced across for the bounding hit, but a third horse, which had appeared along the foul line, kicked up both back legs, and with the bottom of its hooves launched the ball to the deepest part of center garden. It soared over the center scout's head and rolled all the way to the edge of the forest wall. By the time it was relayed back to the infield, Doc stood on second bag with a bases-clearing double.

PILL *and* **ROCK**: *baseball. Also called "rawhide" (see page 12).*

GREEN OASIS: *playing field. Also called the "pitch" (see page 93).*

A third horse kicked up both back legs.

"Lin-dy! Lin-dy!" Ruby chanted.

"That was the most amazing thing ever!" Graham exclaimed.

"Way to strike, Lindy!" Griffith picked up his younger brother and spun him in the air.

"I want to see that again!" Graham declared as Griffith put him down. But the horses had already scampered off the field beyond right garden. "Way to go, Doc!"

Doc Linden tipped his cap to the only three fans cheering for him. In fact, they were the only three cranks saying anything at all. The remainder of the crowd stood in silent shock. Since they hadn't been able to see the horses, all they had seen was a batted ball take a roundabout route to the far limits of the outer garden.

Ruby glanced to Griffith. Once again, she could tell he was wondering the same things she was. Had they done something differently? It wasn't enough to simply hold the baseball, or work together, or believe that things would work out. Maybe they needed all of those ingredients at once in order to help the Travelin' Nine.

"Where did those horses come from?" Graham asked.

"That was the first time they appeared in the top of a frame," Griffith noted.

"That's right," Ruby agreed, taking the baseball back from her younger brother. "Up until now, we've only seen them in the *bottom* of innings."

"Up until now," Graham added, "all we've seen them do is eat grass!"

DAISY CUTTER: *ground ball. Also known as "bug bruiser" (see page 119), "grass clipper," or "ant killer."*

Rube Waddell managed to retire Guy on a daisy cutter to first for the final out of the frame. Nevertheless, the Travelin' Nine had trimmed the lead down to two. With a bounce in their step, they trotted onto the green oasis for the bottom of the sixth.

But unlike when they took the field for the third, fourth, and fifth innings, no horses appeared. This time around, all that could be heard was the unmistakable sound of distant hoof beats.

	1	2	3	4	5	6	7	8	9	R
TN	0	0	0	0	0	3				3
SS	3	2	0	0	0					5

13

★ BEN BRUSH! ★

here are the horses?" Graham hopped back onto the boulder.

Ruby searched for the source of the sounds. "They'll be here," she replied.

Graham held his head. "Why can we hear them, but we can't—"

"Horses!" Ruby exclaimed as they suddenly began to reappear in the outer garden. "I knew they'd be here. And this time, they're the same."

"This time?" Griffith wrinkled his brow.

"Aren't they always the same?"

"No, they're always different." Ruby pointed. "Look at the names."

Griffith went cold. "What . . . what names?"

"Yeah, Ruby." Graham spoke to the field. "What names? The saddlecloths have numbers, but I don't see any names."

Ruby and Griffith looked at one another and then up at Graham. "Numbers?" they asked together.

"You can't see the numbers?" Graham jumped down from the boulder.

Griffith turned back to the field. "The saddlecloths are different colors, but I—"

"Different colors?" Ruby and Graham asked together.

"Red. Yellow. White," Griffith said. "All different colors."

Ruby stared at her older brother. "Do you see what's happening?"

"Obviously not," Griffith replied.

"Me either," Graham added.

"When I look at the horses," Ruby said, holding the ball to her chest, "I can see their names on the saddlecloths. That's how I know they're different. But I don't see numbers or colors. To me, all the saddlecloths are just different shades of gray."

"To me, they're gray with different numbers." Graham took the ball from his sister and cradled it in his hands.

"And I see all different colors," said Griffith.

"Don't you get it?" She smiled as she looked from brother to brother. "This is what Uncle Owen was talking about."

Griffith gasped. " 'See the things that others don't.' "

"Exactly!" Ruby exclaimed.

" 'Things will speak to you.' " Graham pointed at Ruby. " 'In different ways.' "

"Yes!" Ruby said.

"Remember how you said Lindy's hit was the most amazing thing ever?" Griffith motioned to Graham. "We're looking at the same thing and seeing something completely different—now *that's* the most amazing thing ever."

Graham flipped the ball back to Ruby and climbed atop the boulder again. "Next thing you know we'll be seeing unicorns and dragons."

"Dragon!" Ruby leaped. "That's it!"

"What is?" Griffith asked.

Ruby passed the baseball to Griffith, dropped to the ground, and reopened her journal. "The Dragon. That was the name of one of the horses that kicked Lindy's hit. All those horses were from the 1896 Kentucky Derby. Look." She pointed to the names in her journal and read. "The Dragon. Ulysses. Semper Ego."

"But what does that mean?" Griffith sat

"Things will speak to you. In different ways."

down beside her and rested the baseball on the open page. "How does that help us? Or the Travelin' Nine?"

"Check this out." Ruby lifted the baseball still in Griffith's hand and flipped back a page. "These are the horses that ran the Derby in 1895."

"You really did write down the name of *every* horse," Griffith said.

Ruby's smile widened. "Griffy, I take good notes."

"We've been through this already."

"I just want to make sure you don't forget."

"You won't let me."

Ruby patted the open page. "All the horses that ran in the 1895 Derby were the ones on the field in the *fifth* inning. Halma won in '95. That was the horse that kept circling the bases." She turned back another page. "These were all the horses that were out there in the *fourth* inning. They ran the Derby in 1894.

Chant was the horse walking back and forth across the outer garden by Scribe and Crazy Feet."

"Number two." Graham jumped down again.

"With the white saddlecloth," Griffith added.

"But I still don't understand." Graham scratched his head. "How can the horses help?"

Ruby thought for a moment. "When those horses were on the field, all they did was eat grass and walk around. If we had known to look for a certain horse—the winning horse— perhaps something would've happened."

Still holding tightly to the baseball, Griffith studied the action on the field. Happy remained in his groove. He retired the first striker on a cloud hunter to Crazy Feet and set aside the next on a bug bruiser to Bubbles.

CLOUD HUNTER: *fly ball to the outfield or outer garden. Also sometimes referred to as "sky ball" (see page 164), "skyscraper" (see page 164), or "rainmaker."*

BUG BRUISER: *ground ball. Also called "daisy cutter" (see page 111), "grass clipper," or "ant killer."*

119

"I wish I could see the names," Graham said, placing a hand on his brother's shoulder. "How come Ruby can, but we can't?"

"I can't see the numbers, like you can," Griffith said. "Only colors."

"Well, I wish I could see the colors, too."

"You can," Griffith replied.

"No, I can't," Graham answered. "All I can see—"

"In a way, you can," Griffith interrupted. He handed the ball to his brother. "Think back to all those times Dad used to take us to Pimlico Race Course."

"What about it?"

"What color saddlecloth does the horse in the number one post position wear?" Griffith quizzed.

"That's easy. Red."

"Good. And what about the number two position?"

"White." Graham began to nod. "And the

horse that starts from the number three spot wears blue."

Griffith smiled. "So when you see the numbers . . ."

". . . you're really seeing the colors, too!" Graham exclaimed.

But back on the field, things were no longer going as smoothly for Happy. With two outs, the Louisville Nine stroked back-to-back singles, and they now had runners on the corners with their leadoff hitter coming to bat.

"I think the Travelin' Nine could use a little help," Griffith said, rubbing the baseball.

"Let's see if we can create some magic." Ruby glanced down at her journal and then pointed to the scoreboard. "It's the sixth inning."

"Thanks, Ruby." Graham folded his arms. "Who can't see that?"

She guided her brothers a few steps over.

RUNNERS ON THE CORNERS: *When base runners occupy both first base and third base, a team is said to have runners on the corners.*

The crowd had filled in, and she wanted a clearer view of the action.

"Look for the number four horse," she instructed Graham. Then she motioned to Griffith. "Look for the horse with the yellow saddlecloth."

"Is that the horse that won in 1896?" Graham asked. He reached over and joined hands with his brother atop the baseball.

"You got it!" Ruby replied, searching the

field. "I'm looking for Ben Brush. He wasn't one of the horses that helped Lindy's hit in the top of the inning, so I have a feeling—"

"There he is!" Graham pointed toward the ghost horse kicking at the dirt by third base.

"Ben Brush!" Ruby shouted. "C'mon!" She waved to her brothers.

They charged through the cranks, and within seconds all three stood as close to Doc and the hot corner as they could get without stepping onto the field of play.

"Lindy!" Ruby shouted. "The horse!"

"What?" Doc Linden called back; he was playing off the line and over toward short stop.

"*What?*" Graham repeated.

"The horse!" Ruby pointed. "He's the winner. Ride the winning horse!"

"Yes!" Griffith shouted. "Ride the winning horse." He squeezed the baseball as tightly as he ever had and shook it in Doc's direction (but in such a way so that no one could see what he held in his hand).

As the thoroughbred broke toward the third baseline (and as Happy delivered his pitch), Doc Lindy beat his bowlegs and whirled around. Using the skills he'd mastered as a Rough Rider, he lunged for the speeding steed. He grabbed the galloping horse's neck and mane at the very moment the Louisville batter scorched a screamer down the line destined for left garden.

Propelled by the accelerating stallion . . .

Propelled by the accelerating stallion, Doc extended his leather and nabbed the liner! He tumbled to the ground, cradling the ball against his body. Then he scrambled to his knees, pulled the rawhide from his mitt, and raised it high.

"Lin-dy! Lin-dy!" the three Paynes chanted.

Three hands dead!

LINER: *a line-drive batted ball.*

Doc's incredible—*impossible*—catch hushed and humbled the crowd. Total silence greeted the stunned Summer Sluggers as they took their positions for the start of the seventh frame.

Still cupping the baseball, Griffith focused on the fired-up and raring-to-go ballists by the Travelin' Nine bench.

"*Now* let's show a little ginger at the plate!" Doc stormed past his teammates just like he had a few innings earlier.

"Show 'em how we hit!" Woody raised a fist.

"Let's roll, Rough Riders!" Professor Lance urged. "Start us off, Bubbles!"

Bubbles sure did. Leading off the seventh frame, he smacked a double just inside the right field line.

But the Louisville Lightning came right back and fanned both Happy and Crazy Feet. One hand down. Two hands down.

As Tales stepped up to bat, Graham turned to his sister. "Who won the Derby in 1897?" he asked.

Ruby opened her journal again, and when she did, the unmistakable sound of distant hoof beats returned, almost as if the book had let the sounds out.

"Good thinking, Grams." Griffith slapped hands with his brother. "What color am I looking for?" he asked Ruby.

"The winning horse started against the rail."

"That means I'm looking for number one," Graham replied.

"And I'm looking for red," Griffith added.

At that moment, a whole new set of horses started to appear. Some were grazing. Some were trotting. Some were sprinting. All were gathering directly in front of them in foul territory by the left garden line.

	1	2	3	4	5	6	7	8	9	R
TN	0	0	0	0	0	3				3
SS	3	2	0	0	0	0				5

14

★ COMING BACK! ★

rnament. Dr. Catlett." Ruby read the names in her journal and matched them with the horses standing right in front of her. "Goshen. Dr. Shepard."

Griffith inched forward as Tales dug in at the dish. "Where's the horse in red?" he muttered to himself.

"I'm looking for number one," Graham said. He reached across and took the baseball from his brother

"I'm looking for Typhoon II," Ruby said.

"That's his name?" Griffith asked.

Ruby nodded. Her eyes shifted from the thoroughbreds to Tales. The Travelin' Nine's second sack man flapped his elbow four times and awaited the delivery.

Graham raised his arm and held out the ball. "Maybe if I point it at the horses like I did at the scoreboard back in the—"

"Typhoon II!" Ruby suddenly cried.

"Number one!" Graham leaped.

As if the horse heard Ruby's and Graham's calls, the mammoth thoroughbred, sixteen hands in height, charged from the center of the group. It bolted down the foul line, tearing past the cranks behind third bag and the players' bench. The steed headed straight for Tales!

Rube Waddell kicked his leg, reached back, and fired the pill.

Even with a charging horse heading right at him, Tales stood his ground and swung the timber.

Whack!

With Typhoon II only strides away, Tales blasted a daisy cutter toward third and broke from the dish. The third bagger gloved the grounder, just as the stallion skidded into the plate, turned, and burst toward first. It thundered by Tales.

"Grab the reins!" the entire Travelin' Nine bench shouted.

Tales *dove* for the racing horse. He grabbed the side of the saddle, and using every trick he'd learned as a Rough Rider, he allowed the sprinting stallion to pull him down the line. To everyone in Louisville, Tales ran faster than his flailing feet. He crossed the bag milli-moments before the ball.

"*Safe!*" the umpire cried.

Amazed by Tales's mad dash to first, not a single Summer Slugger paid any mind to Bubbles, who had taken off from second with the crack of the bat. Now he was racing toward home!

"*Safe!*" the umpire cried again.

The Travelin' Nine were within one!

Down the first base line, Typhoon II appeared to *smile* at Tales. Then as if to bid the entire team huzzah, the thoroughbred ambled over to the Travelin' Nine bench and bowed. Finally, in a slow and graceful trot, he led all the horses across the green oasis to the trees beyond right garden, where they faded into the afternoon as each stepped into the woods.

Rube Waddell fanned Scribe for the last out of the top of the seventh, but when Louisville came to bat in the home seventh, they couldn't shake off the shock of the Travelin' Nine's speed-of-light base running (or the fact that they had climbed to within one

The thoroughbred ambled over . . .

run). Even without the horses returning to the pitch for the bottom of the frame, Happy set the Summer Sluggers down in order, on a pop-up, a groundout, and a three-pitch strikeout.

However, in the top of the eighth, Rube Waddell was able to regain some of his early-game mastery. He stymied the barnstormer bats, retiring the side in order just like Happy had in the previous inning.

Griffith squeezed the back of his neck. The Travelin' Nine only had one more shot. While the game had gone much better since the horses had arrived, the barnstormers still trailed. Were they missing something? What else were they supposed to do?

He looked to Ruby and Graham, and when he did, he heard Uncle Owen's words in his head.

Be together. Always.

Griffith sighed. How much more together could they possibly be?

He stepped to the edge of the third bag foul line as the Travelin' Nine prepared to take the field in the last of the eighth.

"There's not much left in this tank," Happy said heading to the hill.

"We need you, Happy." Professor Lance patted his shoulder.

"Dig deep, old-timer," Bubbles urged.

Dig deep he did!

Somehow, someway, Happy once again was able to match his counterpart pitch-for-pitch. Of course, it didn't hurt matters that the horses reappeared. Happy and the Travelin' Nine received a little assistance from Plaudit, the winner of the 1898 Derby. Three times the champion thoroughbred allowed a barnstormer to grab its reins in order to record a breathtaking out.

But the Travelin' Nine headed to the ninth still trailing by a run. Once and for all, they were going to need to find a way to solve the problem of the Louisville Lightning.

	1	2	3	4	5	6	7	8	9	R
TN	0	0	0	0	0	3	1	0		4
55	3	2	0	0	0	0	0	0		5

★ THE NINTH INNING ★

s the final frame began, a threatening shadow sliced the field into dark and bright. The sun had shifted, casting a divide between the pitcher's mound and home plate, a line of light and glare. Not only did the Travelin' Nine have to deal with Rube Waddell, but now they also had to deal with Mother Nature.

And those weren't Griffith's only worries. Griffith *felt* eyes upon him. Someone was watching them. When Griffith turned to look, he saw another man in a finely tailored navy suit behind home plate; he also spotted a pink handkerchief in the man's jacket pocket. The man noticed Griffith looking his way and ducked into the crowd.

Griffith blinked hard. Uncle Owen's warning about the Chancellor echoed in his head.

Tapping his forehead with his fist, Griffith turned back to the field. He needed to concentrate on the game, he told himself. Nothing else. There was no longer any doubt that when he, his brother, and sister were working together *and* using the baseball, they helped the Travelin' Nine. And with Guy and Bubbles already taking their warm-up swings in front of the players' bench, Griffith couldn't afford a single distraction.

"All we need is one run," he said, huddling Ruby and Graham in close. "One to tie, two for the lead."

"Let's keep our eyes and ears open," Ruby

Someone was watching them.

urged as Guy stepped to the dish leading off the last.

"Wide open," Graham added.

Unfortunately, their wide-open eyes and ears were drawn to Rube Waddell, who was once again up to his antagonistic antics. En route to the pitcher's hill, the Louisville hurler deliberately detoured into right garden, where the finishing touches were being sprinkled on the postgame meal.

STRIKER'S LINE:
the batter's box. Also known as "striker's box."

"I can taste me vict'ry burgoo!" He strutted past the oversized iron kettles that contained the old Kentucky tradition, the savory stew cooked over an open flame.

"Serve me up a heapin' po'tion." Waddell licked his chops. "Gimme theirs too!" He pointed toward the Travelin' Nine bench. "Can't imagine they'll have much o' an app'tite when I get through with 'em!"

Ruby shook her head.

So did Guy waiting at the striker's line.

By the time Waddell stepped to the hill, she was kicking the batter's box dirt like a rhino ready to rampage. Putting her anger to good use, Guy battled the shadow and belted a single to lead off the frame.

"Next time open your eyes!" Waddell barked at Guy standing on first sack.

Griffith slapped his legs. The Travelin' Nine had needed the leadoff striker to get on base. Guy had done her job.

Bubbles batted next, and he knew better than to even try to challenge the Louisville Lightning. Fortunately, he didn't have to. The situation called for a sacrifice, and Bubbles was the best bunter of the barnstormers. He zeroed in on the first pitch the instant it emerged from the shadow and laid down a textbook one.

"Next time swing the stick!" Waddell called. Then he turned to Guy standing behind him on second bag. "You ain't goin' nowheres."

SACRIFICE: *a hit for the purpose of advancing a runner. In a sacrifice, the batter expects to record an out.*

BUNTER: *a striker, or batter, who makes a soft and short hit, often to advance a runner.*

Now Happy stepped to the striker's line, dragging his timber behind him and looking more exhausted and drained than ever. Under ordinary circumstances, Happy would have had little chance against an ace like Waddell. Under these shadowy conditions, Happy had *no* chance.

ACE: *a star pitcher.*

"Hap-py! Hap-py!" Ruby cheered hopefully.

"C'mon, old-timer!" Griffith clapped.

But Happy's bat never left his shoulder.

Overmatched by the sun, the shadow, and the southpaw, Happy struck out on three straight fastballs.

"Two down, one to go!" Rube Waddell cartwheeled around the mound.

Though the Travelin' Nine were down to their last out, Griffith refused to get discouraged. Perhaps earlier in the game he may have, but no longer. This was baseball, he said to himself; anything was possible. They still had a runner in scoring position

SCORING POSITION: *Any time a runner is on second or third bag, he is considered to be in scoring position.*

with Crazy Feet coming to the plate, and the barnstormers' left scout looked determined to make up for losing the pregame race.

Griffith glanced at Ruby. She lifted the baseball from her pocket, and the moment it emerged, one by one, thoroughbreds began popping up on the infield turf.

"Showtime!" Graham declared as Crazy Feet dug in.

"Yes!" Griffith exclaimed. "What color am I looking for?" he asked his sister.

Ruby passed the ball to Graham and flipped opened her journal. Waddell fired his first flame.

Strike one!

"Who won the Derby in 1899?" Griffith pressed as more horses appeared in the outer garden.

"Manuel," Ruby answered, searching the field. His Lordship grazed behind first, Mazo stood tall in center garden, Fountainbleu paced between third and home, and Corsini paraded out in left. "But I don't see him."

"What number?" Graham whispered.

"One," Ruby answered. "Red."

The Louisville Lightning launched his next offering.

Strike two!

Not only were the Travelin' Nine down to their last out, they were now down to their last strike.

Graham held the ball out to his sister and brother. It shook with his hand. Without saying a word, Ruby placed her hand atop Graham's. Then Griffith placed his upon the other two.

Suddenly a bucking, black thoroughbred appeared behind second bag in short center garden.

"Manuel!" they shouted.

Ruby inserted her pinky into the baseball's hole, and the champion horse—as if responding to their call—charged toward Guy leading off second.

Waddell rocked into his windup. Crazy Feet cocked his bat . . .

"That's the winner!" Ruby yelled.

"Guy!" Griffith screamed to his mother.

As the wife of a Rough Rider, Guy knew all about horses. Without a moment's hesitation, she lunged for the thundering horse's reins. Running alongside the thoroughbred in full gallop, she sped faster than humanly possible, attempting to steal third!

Distracted by the commotion, Waddell *grooved* his next pitch right over the plate, and even as the ball traveled from shade to shine, Crazy Feet could still follow its flight and rotation. He swung and drove it up the middle.

Base hit!

Guy soared around third—propelled by Manuel—and headed for home with the tying run. She unwrapped her wrists from the leather straps and dove for the dish, sweeping her hand across the plate.

"Safe!" the umpire declared.

"Cra-zy Feet! Cra-zy Feet!" Ruby cheered.

"Guy! Guy!" Graham sang.

Guy leaped to her feet and spun around in the air. Then she pretended to tip her cap to her three biggest fans. But she only pretended because she knew better than to lift her hat from her head on the playing field.

Tie game!

She dove for the dish.

16

★ NOW OR NEVER ★

saw his name!" Graham exclaimed. "And the red saddle-cloth, too!"

"So did I!" Ruby hugged her younger brother. "What about you, Griff?" She looked his way.

Griffith was nodding and smiling wider than he had in a long time. With all three of them now able to see the name, number, and saddlecloth color on each horse, he felt more certain than ever that they held the power to help the barnstormers win.

"We still have work to do," Griffith said to

his brother and sister. "We're almost there, but we're not done yet."

"Then let's do it," Graham said. "Who should hold the ball?"

"Let's keep things exactly the same," Ruby replied as Tales stepped to the plate with the potential go-ahead run standing on first bag. "You should."

"Works for me." Graham pounded his chest with his fists.

"The Travelin' Nine are counting on us," Griffith said.

"Like they counted on Daddy?" Graham asked.

"Very much." Griffith nodded. "Like they counted on Daddy." He looked to Ruby. "You ready?"

"You bet," she answered while Tales flapped his elbow at the striker's line.

Graham's hand no longer trembled as he held the ball out. Ruby placed her hand atop

Graham's, and then Griffith placed his upon theirs.

"Time!" Tales suddenly called, lifting a hand from his lumber, waving it to the umpire, and stepping from the line.

"Time is out!" the umpired barked before Rube Waddell delivered the pitch.

Griffith, Ruby, and Graham knew exactly why Tales had made the request. He was seeing what they were. All the horses from the 1899 Kentucky Derby had started marching toward the right side of the infield.

"What do you think they're going to do?" Ruby asked.

"We're about to find out," Griffith replied.

When the horses reached the dirt around the Louisville Nine's second sack man, they stopped. But they left a clear path for Crazy Feet, leading off first. It was almost as if the horses were suggesting to the Travelin'

Nine's base runner that he should prepare for a mad dash.

"Time is in," the umpire declared. He pointed to the plate. "Striker to the line!"

Stepping back to the dish, Tales glanced down the third base line to the three Paynes and twitched his bushy mustache. Then he flapped his elbow four times.

"Here we go!" Graham announced.

Waddell rocked into his windup. Crazy Feet broke from first. Ruby inserted her pinky into the baseball's hole. Tales swung the timber.

Crackle!

Tales's bat shattered. The ball popped high into the air. It was sure to be the final out of the top of the ninth. The Summer Sluggers's second baseman drifted over, while the first bag man and right scout eased in to back up the play.

But then, all of a sudden, every thorough-bred congregated on the right side of the diamond began prancing and bucking and kicking—genie-ing up the dust from the dirt-spotted base paths, just like the breeze had earlier in the game. As the cloud of brown thickened, it drifted in the direction of the ball.

The three fielders shielded their faces and lunged for the ball, but the easy pop-up had transformed into a seeing-eye pop-up. It landed in the middle of the triangle of gloves.

Tales stood safely on first, and because he had taken off with the pitch, Crazy Feet was already digging for third by the time the ball touched turf. Barreling around the bag, he didn't break stride. The right scout picked up the ball and threw home. Scribe motioned wildly for Crazy Feet to slide as the ball popped into the backstop's mitt *before* Crazy Feet reached the dish. Crazy Feet slid

SEEING-EYE POP-UP: *a fly ball that lands safely just beyond two or more fielders, so perfectly placed it's almost as if the ball has eyes.*

BACKSTOP: *catcher. Also called "behind."*

A seeing-eye pop-up

toward the *outside* portion of the plate. The backstop dove for his leg.

"*Safe!*" the umpire cried.

The barnstormers had the lead!

17

★ THREE OUTS TO GO ★

his is it!" Graham announced as
the Travelin' Nine took the field
for the last half of the last frame
and the ghost horses finished strutting into
the woods beyond right garden.

"Three outs to go!" Ruby clapped.

She and her brothers hadn't stopped clap-
ping since the barnstormers pulled ahead.
They even applauded when Woody bounced
to first for the final out of the top of the
ninth.

"Listen," Griffith said, huddling his
brother and sister in close one final time.

"What's happening on the field is happening because of us." He looked at Graham. "And because of your baseball."

Graham smiled.

"Dad is watching over us," Griffith continued.

"I know he is," Ruby added.

Griffith peered out at Happy taking the hill and then back at his siblings. "This is everything Dad always taught us. When we work together, use what we learned, *and* use the baseball, that's when the things on the field help the Travelin' Nine."

"Our family includes the Travelin' Nine, right?" Graham asked.

"Absolutely." Griffith tousled his brother's hair. "The Travelin' Nine are a part of the Payne family."

"Who should hold the baseball?" Ruby asked. "Should we all?"

Griffith stroked his chin. "Let Grammy,"

he said. "He was holding it when the horses appeared in the top of the inning."

"Then let's all three of us cheer as hard as we can for Happy." Ruby cupped a hand over her mouth. "Go get 'em, Happy!"

"Dig deep, old-timer!" Graham cried, copying Bubbles's call from earlier.

Happy knew to keep the ball down and off the plate against the Summer Sluggers' first two strikers. Both men had a lot of pop in their lumber, and if Happy were to leave a pitch up over the strike zone, either one could send it into the trees and tie the game.

POP: *power. Also called "thunder" (see page 73).*

So Happy started the leadoff man with a pitch way outside. He swung anyway, and because he couldn't get good wood on it, he popped a sky-high fly ball straight into the air. Guy circled under it and squeezed the pill in her mitt.

One hand down.

For the second striker, Happy stuck

"No celebrating yet, Grammy."

with his plan—nothing directly over the dish, nothing good to hit. But this time, the Louisville striker didn't swing. He laid off Happy's first down-and-away offering, as well as his second low-and-inside one.

With a count of two balls and no strikes, Happy knew his next pitch needed to be over the plate. And it was—right down the middle. The batter smacked a screamer . . . straight into Bubbles's glove at short stop!

"Two down, one to go," Graham cartwheeled around, just like Rube Waddell had earlier in the inning.

"No celebrating yet, Grammy," Griffith cautioned. "There will be plenty of time for that later."

"Remember what Uncle Owen says about close games." Ruby pointed at Graham. "It ain't over till it's over. And I for one believe it."

She was right.

With two hands down, Happy walked the next batter on four pitches.

And the next.

And the next.

"One to tie! Two to win!" chanted the Louisville cranks.

On the mound, Happy's tired shoulders drooped, and his aching legs wobbled. He even struggled to wipe his brow. How was he possibly going to retire the next striker, none other than Pete "the Old Gladiator" Browning?

Ruby looked to Griffith. Griffith turned to Graham. Graham nodded to Ruby.

All three knew what they *needed* to do.

With both hands, Graham held out the baseball. Ruby rested her hand upon it.

"Be together," Griffith whispered as he placed his hand over theirs. "Always."

Ruby inserted her pinky into the odd, acorn-size hole. "Happy could use some horses to help him out."

Graham nodded once. "Then they'll be here."

As one, they watched Happy size up the fearsome striker. Using every ounce of remaining strength, he windmilled his arm and *underhanded* the pitch.

Crack!

Horses, horses, but *not* everywhere!

Instead, they appeared charging off the left garden line as if they were bursting out of a starting gate. . . .

A towering sky ball soared toward deep right garden. . . .

SKY BALL: *fly ball to the outfield or outer garden. Also sometimes referred to as "cloud hunter" (see page 119), "skyscraper" (see below), or "rainmaker."*

SKYSCRAPER: *fly ball to the outfield or outer garden. Also sometimes referred to as "cloud hunter" (see page 119), "sky ball" (see above), or "rainmaker."*

Ruby pulled her hand off the ball, whirled around, and leaped onto the boulder. "Thrive! His Excellency! Florizar!" She read off the names she could make out.

"Kentucky Farmer! Highland Lad! Hindus!" Griffith announced. "Who are these horses?"

"I've never seen *any* of them *anywhere!*" Ruby pulled her hair with both hands as the horses tore past Crazy Feet.

Out in right field, blinded by the shadows and sun, Woody gave chase, racing toward where the ball *might* be headed. Farther and farther the skyscraper sailed. Woody shielded his eyes as he sped toward the deepest corner of right garden. . . .

The horses jockeyed for position as they blazed across the outer garden and blew by Scribe. . . .

"Down the stretch they come!" Graham called, echoing the umpire's words from the pregame race. He lifted Griffith's hand, and Graham inserted *both* of his tiny pinkies into the hole.

Suddenly Ruby spotted another horse in the herd.

Lieutenant Gibson.

She couldn't believe her eyes. That was the name she'd seen next to the slot for the winner of *next year's* Kentucky Derby.

"Lieutenant Gibson!" she shouted louder than everyone in Louisville put together.

At that moment, the speeding thoroughbred emerged from the pack, racing faster than any Kentucky Derby champion ever had. He headed straight for Woody.

"Woody!" Graham yelled. "Number three!"

But Lieutenant Gibson bucked wildly . . .

"The blue horse!" Griffith cried.

Woody laid out for the charging horse. He reached for the reins and grabbed on. . . .

But Lieutenant Gibson bucked wildly, launching Woody like a slingshot. . . .

Woody sailed through the air *faster* than the baseball. It landed in his outstretched leather an instant before ball and body met earth.

"Third hand out!" the umpire cried. "The Travelin' Nine triumph!"

For certain, the Louisville ballists and their cranks would talk about Woody's miraculous catch for generations. No one had ever seen a grab quite like it (nor would they ever again).

Griffith, Ruby, Graham, and the Travelin' Nine stormed the field. In the deepest corner of right garden, they piled into a victorious heap.

"We won!" Graham celebrated, perched

atop the mountain of bodies. He raised the baseball high over his head, and since all the barnstormers were underneath him, none of them saw.

So he thought.

★ THE VICTORY BURGOO ★

n a surprising display of sportsmanship and respect, Rube Waddell was the first to congratulate the Travelin' Nine on their hard-fought victory. In fact, the Louisville Lightning bounced from bleachers to backstop, assembling and arranging the postgame meal.

"May I have your attention, please?" Waddell requested of all who gathered in right garden. "May I have your attention, please?"

"What does he want *this* time?" Graham asked, sucking his teeth.

"I think we may be pleasantly surprised," Ruby replied, her blue eyes sparkling.

Rube Waddell waited for the din to die down. Then he pulled a paper from his pocket and raised a glass high.

"Ahem," he cleared his throat. "Ahem, ahem!" Finally he began his toast:

> *"Baseball has provided*
> *a most mem'rable Saturday.*
> *Loo-uh-vul-lans will always*
> *   treasure*
> *watchin' the Travelin' Nine play.*
>
> *'Course, we Summer Sluggers*
> *would have preferred a diff'rent*
> *   final score.*
> *Still we salute our fellow patriots*
> *who served so admirably in the war.*
>
> *Now speakin' for meself,*
> *sometimes my eyes did deceive.*

Those divin' catches and flyin' ballists
were sights quite hard to believe.

Once I thought I heard hoofbeats
beside me on the mound.
But when I looked about
I could find no horse around.

As for my antics on the diamond,
I meant no dishonor or mockery.
I did not intend ill-sportsmanship
toward such a respected adversary.

But when I play this perfect game,
my excitement I cannot contain.
So kindly excuse any behaviors;
I was only wishin' to entertain.

"In sum," Rube Waddell concluded, "I say
to one and all: Hip . . . hip . . . huzzah!"

"Hip . . . hip . . . huzzah!" all the ballists
toasted.

As afternoon turned to evening, the Travelin' Nine, the Summer Sluggers, and the scores that remained savored the festive postgame meal.

Well, not everyone *savored*.

"You expect me to eat that?" Graham pretended to gag.

"Grammy." Griffith elbowed his brother hard. "Don't be impolite."

"I'm not being impolite. I'm being honest. Do you know what that looks like?"

Griffith elbowed him a second time. "Burgoo contains stuff you like—beef, pork, chicken, mutton. It also has lots of vegetables—peas, tomatoes, corn, potatoes, lima beans, okra."

"Okra?"

Griffith sighed. There was little use in arguing, because even Griffith had to concede that the burgoo didn't exactly look fit for human consumption.

But finally, both boys caved and braved

the new food, and much to their surprise, they loved it—so much so that Ruby had to pry Graham's bowl from his fingers when he lined up for a *fourth* helping.

Griffith wiped the sweat from his temples as he watched the two men head off.

He had spotted them standing behind the tally board by home plate during the Louisville Lightning's speech. Then as the ballists and cranks had dined, he had noticed them again, trying to blend in while they *hovered* near the Professor, Tales, and Woody.

Of all the individuals that had stayed after the match, these two men were the only ones who chose not to participate in any of the festivities.

Griffith hadn't imagined any of it. He really had caught these men watching them today.

The sweat continued to pour down

MATCH: *a baseball game or contest.*

175

Griffith's face because he knew exactly who these men were and why their impeccable suits with the pink pocket squares looked so familiar. That's what the men had worn at the market that day last fall. They were the Chancellor's men.

Ruby, Graham, and he were being followed.

Griffith looked over at his mother, sitting with Doc, Bubbles, and some ballists from the Louisville team. Ruby had been with the group, but now she was heading out toward left garden, where Scribe was seated by himself.

Griffith exhaled. *This* could no longer wait. He hurried across the field.

"I'm sorry to interrupt," he said as he approached the group of adults.

"Come join us, young man," Bud Hillerich said, brushing the turf to his left. "We're talking baseball, and from what I hear, you're the resident expert."

"Thank you, sir." Griffith managed a smile. "But for the moment, I must decline." His face went grim as he turned to Guy and looked her in the eye. "I need to talk to you. In private."

19

★ SCRIBE SHARES ★

ou weren't frightened of the horses," Ruby said to Scribe.

"No." He shook his head. "None of the Rough Riders were."

Ruby had joined Scribe on the grass in the deepest part of left garden because she was looking for answers. She wanted to know what he thought of all the strange things that had happened on the field during the game.

"The horses helped," she stated.

"They most certainly did." Scribe tucked his quill behind his ear. "What we don't understand is *why*."

"What do you mean?" Ruby flipped the hair from her neck.

Scribe smiled his soft smile. "They helped. Yes." He spoke in bursts. "But in Cuba, when the unusual occurred, we had your father. And his baseball. Here, we have neither."

Ruby swallowed. "Daddy's with us. He's making sure we're safe."

"Which is why we listen. We trust the three of you like we trusted him."

Ruby reached over and patted Scribe's leather-bound journal. "Can I read what you wrote?"

Scribe shook his head once.

"Please," Ruby said. "I love the way you write."

"I've only jotted a few reflections," Scribe said.

Ruby tilted her head. "Scribe, I'm sure whatever you've written is beautiful."

He looked at Ruby's journal, resting in

The largest human being she had ever seen

her lap. "Can I read what *you've* written?" he asked.

"No!" She covered it with both arms. "It's private."

"I see." Scribe smiled his soft smile. "You want to read what I've written, but I'm forbidden to read what you have. Somehow that doesn't seem fair."

"Sounds fair to me." Ruby smiled back.

She loved spending time with Scribe. They talked about so many things. Even the war. Scribe had shared with her things about Cuba that not even her own father had told her.

Most of what he shared started in his writings. Scribe was a man of few words. Because speech did not come easily to him, he spoke deliberately, and the sentences he did manage to piece together often sounded rehearsed.

Ruby stared into the eyes of the largest human being she had ever seen. Even sitting down, he was enormous. Graham could stand next to him when he was seated and *still* be looking up at him. From time to time, Graham called him the Silent Giant, but Ruby wished he wouldn't. Scribe already had a nickname: Scribe. It was perfect. It was plenty.

"Can't I read just one thing?" Ruby reached over and traced her fingers along the binding of his journal. She looked at him with her deep blue eyes. "Please."

Scribe sighed. "You're not going to take no for an answer, are you?"

Ruby shook her head.

"Very well." He removed the quill from behind his ear and brushed the feathers across the open page. "I'll read you what I've written."

"Thank you, Scribe."

He shifted over so that they both could view the words in his leather-bound record. "It's not much, my young lady friend," he said. "Most of it will make little or no sense at all. At this point, it's notes and thoughts. My true writing will take place tonight."

Then, in his gentle and reassuring voice, he read:

"The speed at which fortunes can change never ceases to astound.

"As dusk arrives this August day, I write with renewed optimism. What a glorious victory! A testament to the valor and nobility of the Travelin' Nine.

"We will succeed. We must succeed.

"I look toward those three precious children, and sadly, I journey to parts so dark. How little they do know. Alas, even if they did, could they comprehend? Do we

*comprehend? We are men who have
faced the horrors of war and turned
death from our doorsteps. Yet none
of us could know how we would fare
under such grave conditions.*

"We will succeed. We must succeed.

*"Look out, Chicago, here come the
Travelin' Nine!"*

Ruby felt a chill rush through her. "What parts so dark?" she asked.

Scribe shook his head.

"What grave conditions?" she pressed.

Still, he didn't respond.

Ruby knew Scribe well enough to stop asking; he would provide no answers now.

"That was beautiful." She reached across and closed his journal. "Thank you, Scribe." Then she leaned over and hugged him.

"Thank you," he said.

"I need to head back over to the others."
She stood up and gestured to Graham, dart-
ing around the base paths. "I think it's time
he returns to the hostel."

★ THE ABSOLUTE TRUTH ★

need to ask you something, Mom," Griffith said, leading her across the outer garden, away from the players and rooters.

"I know you do."

"You do?"

"Of course, I do." She tucked a dangling strand of hair back into her cap. "It's the same question you've been asking. The one I haven't really answered."

Griffith shook his head. "It's more than that now, Mom. It's a lot of questions. We're being—"

Elizabeth reached over and placed two fingers on her son's lips. "It's only one question, Griff. It all comes back to that same question. Why are the Travelin' Nine *really* barnstorming?"

"Why won't you tell me? I know more than you think."

"I see that." Elizabeth's grim expression matched Griffith's. "And that's why it's time for me to tell you. We're barnstorming because we need to raise money. We made a good amount today. Several hundred dollars and—"

"I know all that, Mom. But what I—"

"Let me speak, Griff," she interrupted. "This is hard for me, and I wasn't intending on doing it now. So just bear with me. I will tell you everything. I promise. The absolute truth."

Griffith stared up at his mother. The last time he had seen her face so filled with anguish had been a month earlier in Uncle Owen's backyard.

"What I'm about to tell you"—she spoke slowly—"will be very difficult to hear, and I'd prefer if you didn't share it with your sister and brother. I don't want—especially Grammy—I do not want him to know of this."

Griffith nodded.

Elizabeth swallowed. "Your Uncle Owen has made some mistakes. Big mistakes. I didn't learn of them—any of them—until the night of Daddy's funeral. That's why Uncle Owen and I fought like we did that evening."

Griffith opened his mouth to speak, but she shook her head.

"He owes money. An enormous sum to the bank. And I believe he owes to others as well."

"Mom, we're being followed," Griffith blurted.

"Who's following us?"

"The Chancellor."

"Griffith Payne!" Elizabeth shook her head. "The Chancellor isn't involved. Your uncle would've warned me if he was."

"He is."

"No, Griff. And don't ever say such a thing. I know this has been difficult on you three, but he's not following us."

"Mom, I . . ."

Griffith stopped himself. She was wrong. He knew she was wrong, and it frustrated him—even angered him—that she was being so dismissive. But there was no sense in arguing. He couldn't exactly show her the letter because of the warning on the back. And at this moment, she could only focus on what she had to tell him.

"Our family is in peril," Elizabeth continued. "We're all at risk. That's why the Rough Riders have banded together like they have. For us. For Daddy." She glanced to the heavens. "Griff, Uncle Owen is responsible for this danger. He didn't say so, but he didn't have to. Some things you just know."

Some things you just know.

The words reverberated in Griffith's head, and at that moment, all of his hunches were confirmed.

They *were* being followed. There was no longer a shred of doubt left in his mind— even if his mother couldn't believe it.

This was about Graham. He was the one in the greatest danger of all.

And the Chancellor or his men had done something to Uncle Owen. That's why the letter had arrived looking like it had.

Griffith closed his eyes for a moment. At least he, his sister, and his brother had figured out the baseball. It brought him comfort. And they had managed to keep it from everyone too. Just like Uncle Owen had told them.

He opened his eyes. Griffith had learned the absolute truth, and part of that truth was realizing that he knew far more than about the dangers, about *everything*, than his mother did. It was time to trust *all* his instincts.

Some things you just know.

"I know you have many questions." Elizabeth squeezed Griffith's hands. "I'll answer all of them. I'll tell you everything

I know. Every last detail. On the train to Chicago . . ."

The sight of Ruby and Graham charging across the field in their direction ended her sentence.

"You'd better come over," Graham said. "They're getting ready to serve dessert."

"Dessert?" Elizabeth laughed. "Haven't you had enough to eat?"

"That's what I told him," Ruby said.

"We should join the others." Elizabeth touched Griffith's cheek. "But before we do, I want to say something to all of you."

"What is it?" Graham asked.

She drew her children in close. "I was very proud of the three of you today. The Travelin' Nine couldn't have won without you."

"We felt like we were part of the team," Graham said.

"We *are* part of the team," Ruby added.